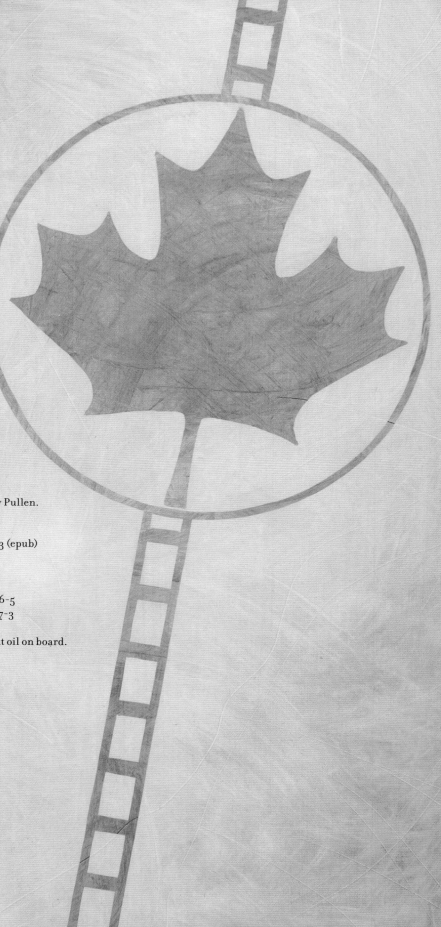

For my family, with love

—Z.H.

Published in Canada and the United States of America
by Tundra Books, a division of Random House of
Canada Limited, a Penguin Random House Company

Library of Congress Control Number: 2014951816

Library and Archives Canada Cataloguing in Publication

Hyman, Zachary, author
      Hockey hero / by Zachary Hyman ; illustrated by Zachary Pullen.

Issued in print and electronic formats.
ISBN 978-1-77049-630-9 (bound).—ISBN 978-1-77049-632-3 (epub)

      I. Pullen, Zachary, illustrator II. Title.

PS8615.Y527H63 2015   jC813'.6   C2014-906436-5
                                               C2014-906437-3

The artwork in this book was rendered in oil paint and walnut oil on board.
The text was set in Filosofia.

www.penguinrandomhouse.ca

Printed and bound in China

1 2 3 4 5 6   20 19 18 17 16 15

TUNDRA BOOKS | Penguin Random House

There's something special about a cold winter day,
when raindrops turn to snowflakes and rippled water chills to ice.

On that kind of day, there's no better feeling than strapping on a pair of worn skates and cutting across smooth, clear ice with sharp blades of steel. Add a black rubber puck and a banged-up old stick, and something special turns into something magical … hockey!

Eight-year-old Tommy Toomay grew up in a hockey family. His two older brothers both played, and Tommy's grandfather won a Stanley Cup with the world-famous Detroit Red Wings. And now Grandpa had the coolest job in the world, working at the Hockey Hall of Fame.

Everyone naturally thought that Tommy would become a hockey player too. Everyone except Tommy, that is. You see, Tommy Toomay was extremely shy. In fact, Tommy was so shy that every time he spoke, he stuttered. Kids called him "Two-Times Tommy" because whenever he got nervous, he stuttered each syllable two times.

Every evening and all weekend long, Tommy's parents dragged him from rink to rink to watch his two brothers play. Tommy was always the first one through the door. He'd pull out a clipboard and a pen and head for the stands, where he'd sit for hours, recording facts and figures. Tommy knew the stats of every kid who'd ever played hockey in the Little NHL.

Yep, Tommy sure loved hockey, but no matter how hard his parents tried, he *always* refused to play.

Tommy's brother Billy played for the Hamilton Red Wings,
a hockey club with a long history of developing young players.
He was the team captain and the leading scorer, and nobody
dared tease Tommy when Billy was around.

Tommy looked up to his brother, who was everything
he wished he could be. But even so, when Tommy's parents
signed him up to play on the Red Wings too, he said no.
He never once played or practiced with the team.

Every chance Tommy had, he visited his grandfather at the Hockey Hall of Fame. They spent hours together, exploring every magic inch of that perfect place. "Hockey legends live forever in these halls," Grandpa always said. "Memories and dreams—that's what hockey's all about."

As Grandpa rattled off tales of wonder and excitement, Tommy stared in awe at the displays of hockey's most legendary players—including "Number Four" Bobby Orr, Maurice "Rocket" Richard and "Mr. Hockey" himself, Gordie Howe.

"Bobby Orr was the most graceful skater I ever saw," said Grandpa. "He was as fast as the wind. Rocket Richard had hands of gold, and he filled the net with pounds of pucks. And Gordie Howe ... well, he was my favorite player of all time! He had the heart of a lion—and the sharpest elbows in the league." Grandpa rubbed his shoulder, having been on the receiving end of a couple of Gordie's best.

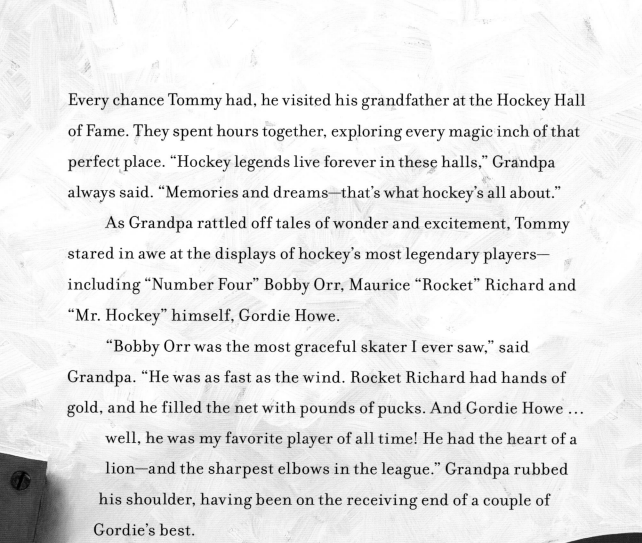

Grandpa always believed that Tommy was special, and he knew that special quality would shine bright someday, when Tommy was ready.

    While everyone focused on Billy, Grandpa took Tommy to a frozen pond and taught him to skate, shoot, pass and play. "You gotta have fun! Bobby Orr used to say he was the happiest guy in the world when he was on the ice."

    Whenever Tommy got tired of practicing, Grandpa encouraged him to keep going. "Gordie Howe always worked like a bull and never quit," he declared. "'One hundred percent is all we ask!' he'd say."

    When it came to goals, Grandpa would bring up the great Rocket Richard. "He scored lotsa goals, and do you know why? Because he shot the puck! He once said, 'Fifty percent of goals are luck. You have to work for the others.' So shoot, shoot and shoot some more!"

As the cold winds started to warm, the hockey season melted away. Billy's team won the league final and advanced to the city championship. Winning that game was a Toomay family tradition!

When the big day finally arrived, Coach Guy scribbled Tommy's name on the roster, just as he did every game, even though the boy never played.

As the two teams warmed up, Tommy took his usual seat in the stands. Reaching into his bag, he pulled out his clipboard and his big blue pen. He drew two columns for goals and assists and a box for shots taken and face-offs won. Tommy made sure his writing was nice and neat, just as his teacher, Mrs. Flanders, had taught him.

Some local kids saw him and started heckling. "Look, it's brainless, boring Tommy Toomay!" roared one. Another bully jeered, "It's T-t-two T-t-times T-t-tommy!" Then they all laughed and threw popcorn at him. Tommy ignored them—even though it hurt inside.

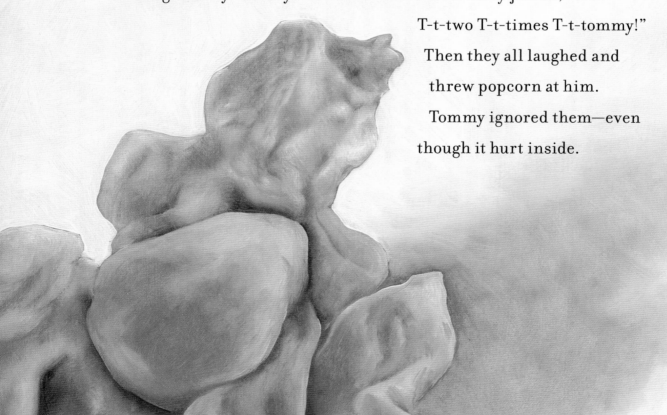

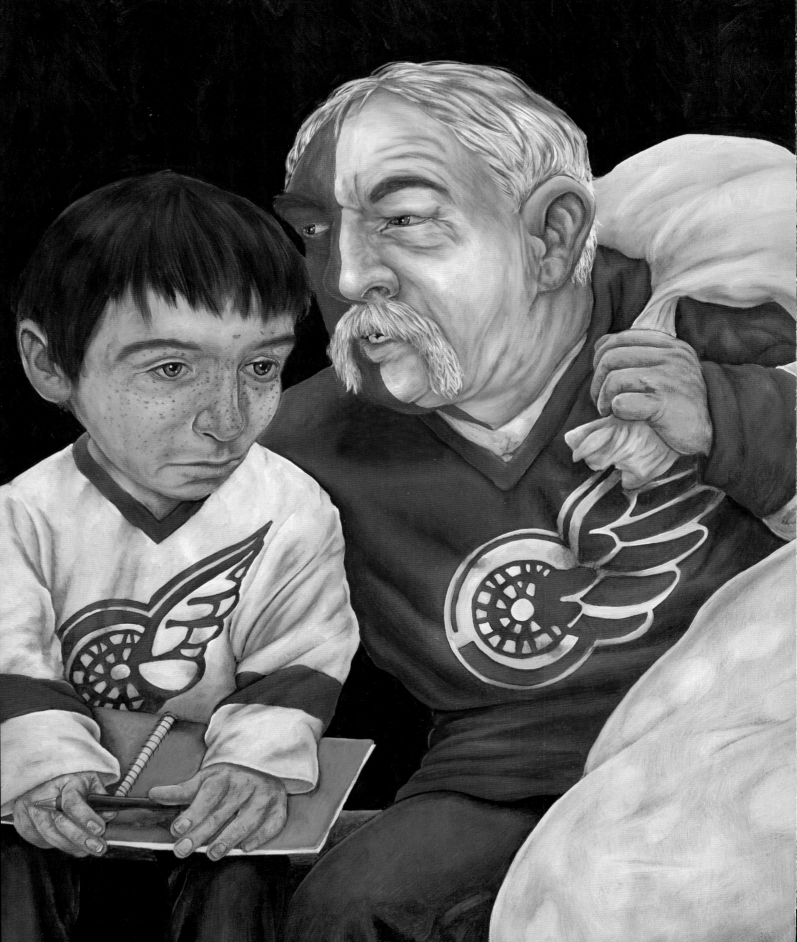

"Scram!" barked Grandpa.

The rowdy kids scattered like a pack of wolves.

He turned to Tommy. "Don't worry about them. They're just jealous."

"Of what?" asked Tommy.

"Of you, kiddo! You're special."

"No, I'm not," murmured Tommy, lowering his head.

"Sure you are. You just have to believe in yourself." Grandpa looked him square in the eye. "Listen, Tommy, we make our destiny every day. You gotta set your own goals, take your shots and make them come true."

Grandpa smelled like roasted chestnuts and cedar wood chips—a smell Tommy would remember for the rest of his life. He was decked out in a Red Wings jersey, and his face was painted red and white.

"Should be a good one tonight, eh, Tommy boy?"

Grandpa carefully tucked a big white garbage bag under his seat. Everyone—including Tommy—knew exactly what was inside.

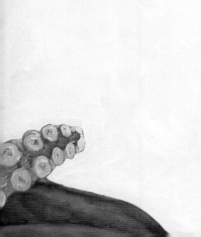

Grandpa was a pretty normal grandparent—until a hockey game erupted. Then he never sat still. He sizzled and smoked and blew his top like a volcano! He hollered and howled, yelled and yowled, bubbling over the seats like fiery lava!

Grandpa loved to irritate the referees, the opposing fans and the players on the other team. Last season he was banned for throwing an octopus on the ice every time Billy scored—and Billy scored a lot!

This game pitted the Red Wings against the Junior Canadiens. It was a fierce rivalry. The Wings were small, skilled and fast. The Canadiens were large and dangerous.

By the end of the first period, the Red Wings were winning 2–1. Billy had scored both goals, and Grandpa was hurling octopuses like a baseball pitcher. They were landing everywhere—even on the referee's head!

The second period was rough and tough. The Canadiens went on the offensive, and tensions boiled over. Grandpa kept reaching into his bag, flinging octopus after octopus at the ice. He was snarling and barking like a rabid dog. Tommy could have sworn that his wild white mane had turned a fiery red.

Finally, the second period came to a close. The Canadiens were winning 3–2.

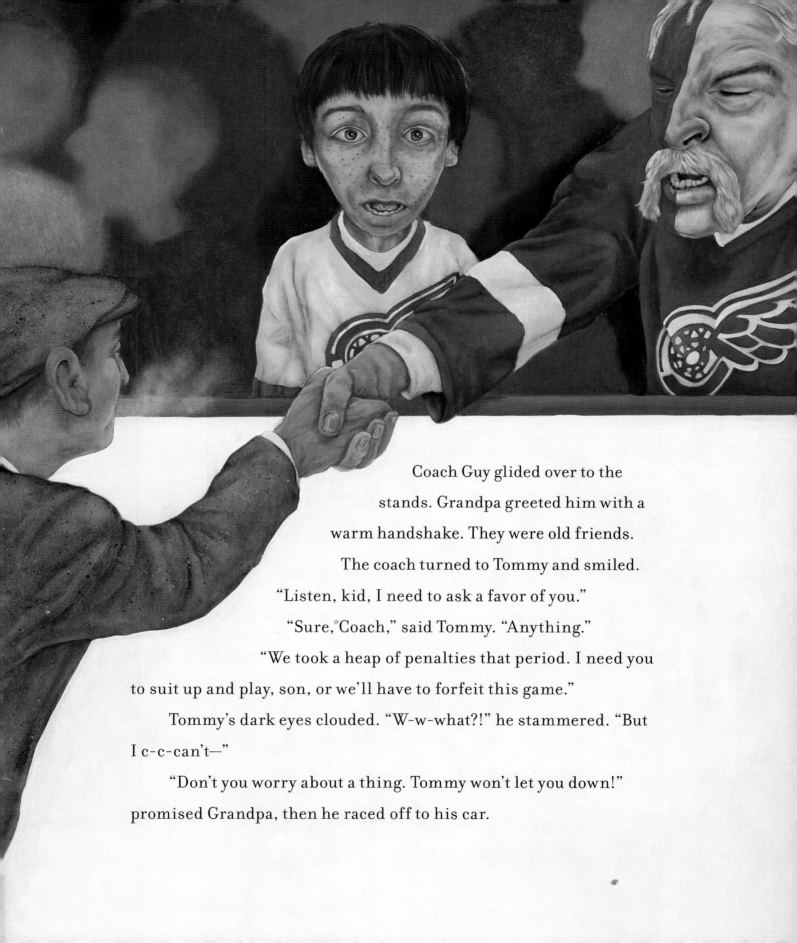

Coach Guy glided over to the
stands. Grandpa greeted him with a
warm handshake. They were old friends.
The coach turned to Tommy and smiled.
"Listen, kid, I need to ask a favor of you."
"Sure, Coach," said Tommy. "Anything."
"We took a heap of penalties that period. I need you
to suit up and play, son, or we'll have to forfeit this game."

Tommy's dark eyes clouded. "W-w-what?!" he stammered. "But
I c-c-can't—"

"Don't you worry about a thing. Tommy won't let you down!"
promised Grandpa, then he raced off to his car.

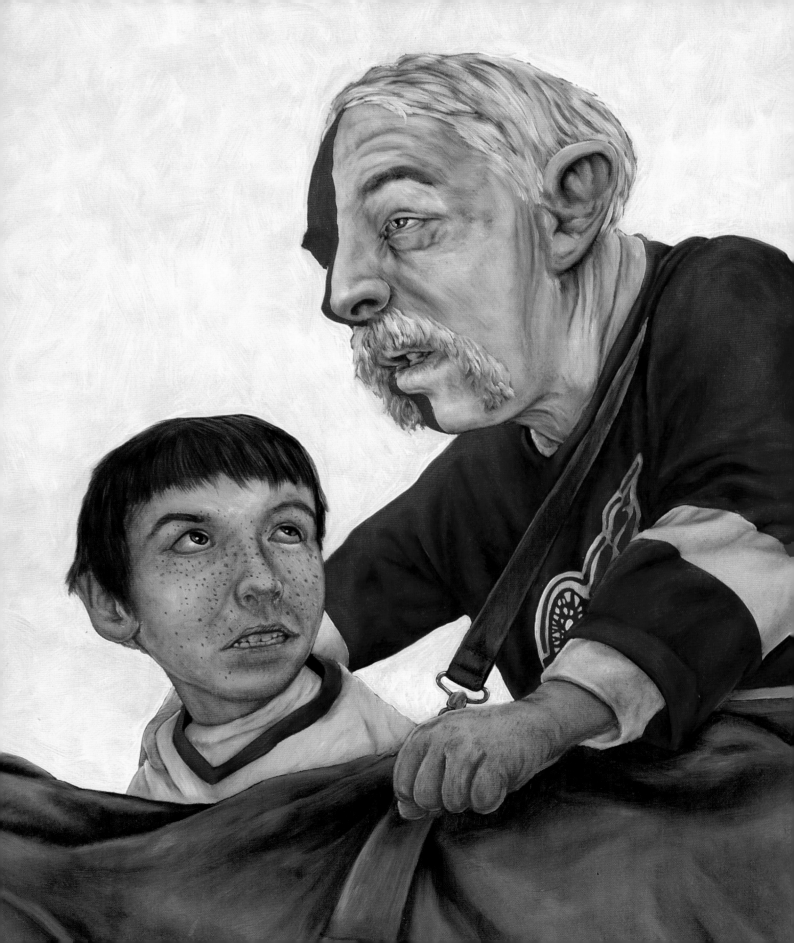

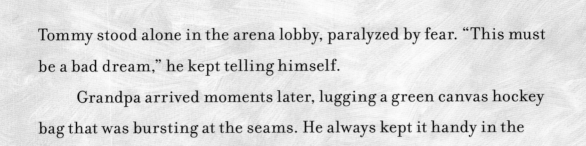

Tommy stood alone in the arena lobby, paralyzed by fear. "This must be a bad dream," he kept telling himself.

Grandpa arrived moments later, lugging a green canvas hockey bag that was bursting at the seams. He always kept it handy in the trunk of his car, just in case. And this was that "just in case"!

Grandpa wrapped his arm around Tommy and led him toward the Red Wings dressing room. "Don't worry, kiddo. I brought you a bag full of splendid surprises!"

Tommy was so nervous his teeth were chattering.

As they entered the dressing room, Billy stood up and greeted Tommy with a high-five. "Hey, little brother! Let's give 'em heck!"

Tommy panicked and turned to run. There was no way he was going to suit up and play. The Canadiens were barbarians!

Coach Guy blocked the exit. He spun the youngest Toomay back toward the team and announced, "Boys, Tommy Toomay's gonna lead us to the cup!"

No one said a word …

Billy gave Tommy a cheerful punch in the arm. "My little brother's the best-kept secret in hockey, and he'll bring us glory, you'll see!"

The Red Wings erupted in a cheer, chanting, "Beat 'em, bust 'em—that's our custom!" as Billy led them onto the ice for the third period warm-up.

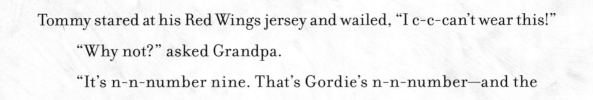

Tommy stared at his Red Wings jersey and wailed, "I c-c-can't wear this!"

"Why not?" asked Grandpa.

"It's n-n-number nine. That's Gordie's n-n-number—and the Rocket's!"

Grandpa grinned. "And now it's yours too!"

Tommy plopped down on a bench and let out an unhappy sigh. Grandpa bent over and began to unzip his old canvas hockey bag.

"When I was your age there was a frozen pond near my house too, and we played shinny every day and all night long. Ma had to drag me off the ice by my ear. That's why I have such big long ears!"

"Hairy ears!" teased Tommy, watching in wide-eyed amazement as the zipper slid down its track. He could have sworn he saw sparkles!

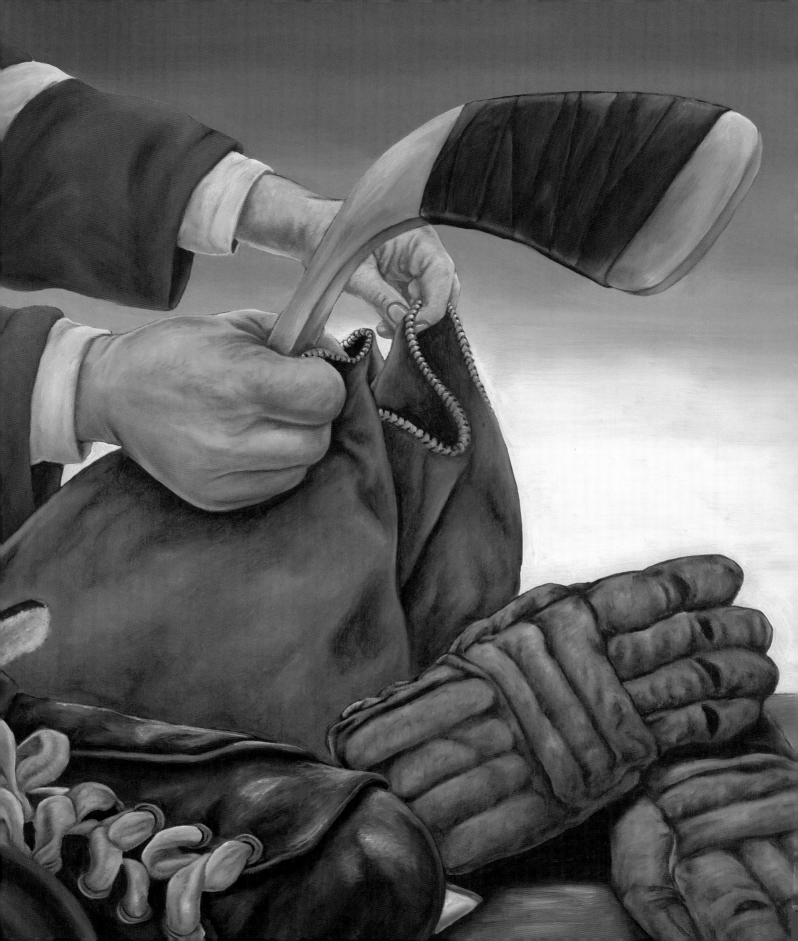

Tommy was soooo rattled. He felt as hollow as a slice of Swiss cheese. "Grandpa, w-w-what am I g-g-gonna do?"

"You're gonna play some hockey, kiddo!" Grandpa patted him gently on the shoulder. "This is a wonderful opportunity."

"Yeah, an opportunity to g-g-get creamed," Tommy replied.

"Enough of that talk! We both know you can play. In fact, you're probably the best player I ever taught."

"I'm the only p-p-player you ever t-t-taught!"

Grandpa scratched his head. "Well, that's true … but I have faith in you. And I've also got something special to help you out."

He reached into his battered old bag and pulled out a pair of leather skates, two beat-up hockey gloves and a tattered old twig of a stick.

Tommy stared at the items in disbelief. "Are t-t-those what I think they are?"

Grandpa chuckled. "Yep! Bobby Orr's last pair of skates, Rocket Richard's famous leather gloves and Gordie Howe's record-breaking stick."

"But, Grandpa, I can't use these!"

"Sure you can. They were good enough for the legends, and they're good enough for you! C'mon, I'll help you get dressed. We'll have you out on that ice lickety-split!"

As the third period warm-up ended, the referee skated over to the Red Wings bench. "Listen, Coach, you got two minutes until I call this game and you forfeit," he scolded. "Where's your extra player?"

Grandpa opened the dasher door and snarled, "He's right here!" Then he turned to Tommy with a mighty grin. "Go on, kiddo! Show 'em all what ya got!"

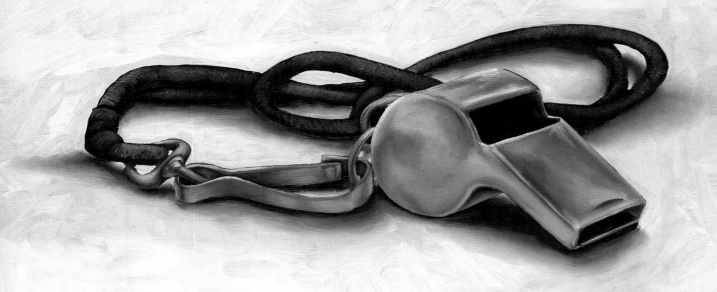

Tommy hopped onto the ice—and fell flat on his bum!

The bullies laughed and jeered. "Ha, ha, Two-Times Tommy! Do it again, you donkey! Hee-haw! Hee-haw!"

Grandpa wasn't amused. He called out to Tommy, "It's not how you fall down, kiddo—it's how you stand back up."

Just then, the fans started clapping. They rose to their feet, chanting the boy's name: "Tom-my, Tom-my, Tom-my ..."

Slowly, he lifted his head and got back up on his skates.

His mom waved and blew him a giant kiss from the stands.

Tommy was so embarrassed.

Coach Guy corralled his players. "C'mon, boys. We're down by only one goal. Let's get it back!"

The referee blew his whistle. "We ain't got all day, eh!" he grumbled.

Tommy lined up for the face-off against Tug McGrail, the biggest, toughest, meanest player in the league.

"I'm gonna squash you like a bug!" said Tug, breathing down on Tommy.

"You gotta catch me first!" gulped Tommy, wishing he had real wings.

The crowd was completely caught up in the game. The Red Wings fans were all pumped up, cheering, "We're red, we're white, we're really dy-na-mite!" And Grandpa was the loudest of them all.

When the puck dropped, Tommy zoomed away from Tug. He remembered what Grandpa had taught him. He took long, smooth strides across the ice. Bobby Orr's skates were really big and clunky, but the shiny black leather was well worn and comfortable. Tommy's skating was fluid and fast—maybe even as graceful as Bobby's! He felt light on his feet and soft in his hands, like Rocket Richard. His body tingled with excitement as time ticked off the clock without a goal.

With two minutes left in the game, Tommy parked in front of the opposing net. He watched as Billy fired a wicked slap shot from the blue line … but the goalie saved it with the tip of his stick.

Rebound!

The puck bounced right in front of Tommy. He flicked his wrist quickly, sending the hard rubber disk off his stick just like Gordie Howe.

The red light lit up—Tommy had scored!

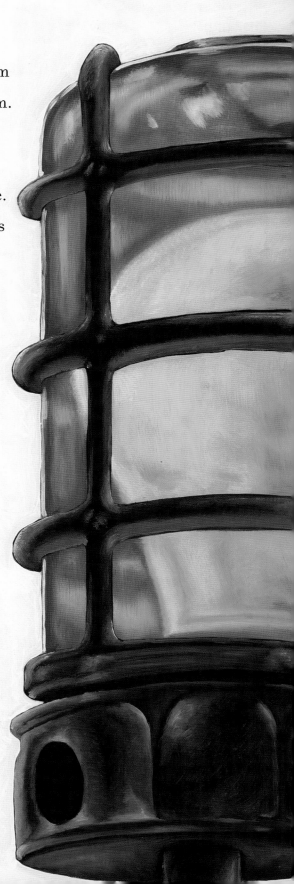

"Holy Toledo! That must have gone a hundred miles an hour!" declared one referee to another. "That kid's got cannon!"

Tommy had tied the game. His teammates hugged him. It made him feel so good inside, like he belonged and was part of a family.

And Tug McGrail … well, he didn't look so big anymore.

"That's my boy! That's my Tommy!" hollered Grandpa as he reached into his bag and flung a giant octopus onto the ice.

The crowd roared with excitement.

The play continued. The Canadiens were all over the Red
Wings, buzzing their net like bees in a hive. Coach
Guy called a time-out. The score was tied 3–3.
"Boys, I'm proud of you. You're having
fun, and you're hanging in with a short bench.
Let's dump it down the ice and head for overtime."

"But, Coach," said Tommy, "what if
we score?"

Coach Guy scratched his head.
The puck was deep in their zone with
only *nine* seconds left. "Tell you what,
kid—you score and they'll never forget
you!" He pointed to the stands. "You'll
be a real-life legend!"

Both teams lined up for the face-off. Billy won the draw, chipping the puck back to his little brother. Tommy wound up and blasted the rubber biscuit across the ice …

SWOOSH!

The Canadiens goalie never even saw it. No one saw it. All that remained of the puck were some melted rubber pieces splattered across the white boards behind the net. Tommy had scored again!

Grandpa turned to the bullies and shouted, "Two-Times Tommy cuz he scores TWO TIMES!"

Then everybody tossed popcorn at *them*!

The buzzer sounded, ending the game. The Red Wings won the championship cup that incredible day in May!

As they sat in the dressing room, Grandpa helped Tommy get changed.
He put away his "special gear" piece by piece.

When Grandpa zipped up the old canvas hockey bag, Tommy
could have sworn he saw sparkles ...

Grandpa turned to him and said, "You know, kiddo, the magic
wasn't really in this old equipment."

Tommy smiled.

"I know, Grandpa—
the magic was
in *me*!"

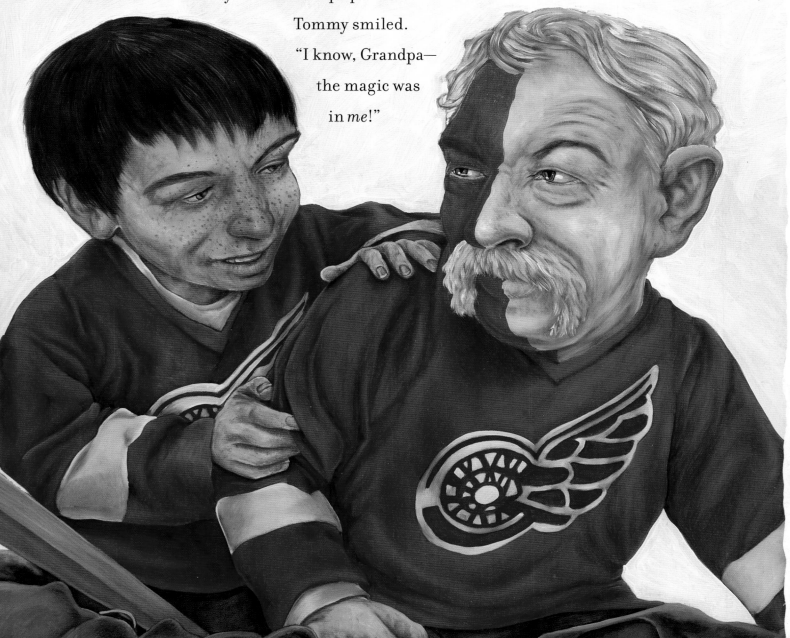